Moira and the Magnificent Bee Beds

Written and Illustrated by Nan Eshelby

"Do you make your bed
with a duvet and sheet?

Why don't you use mud?
Squash it under your feet.

The furry red mason bee
makes beds out of mud.

But you couldn't use them;
you'd fall out with a thud."

Maisie Daisy & Mo
Nature Books

Maisie, Daisy, and Mo
were relaxing in the sunshine
and Daisy was reading
aloud from her book.

"Wow! A mud bed,
that sounds a strange book, Daisy,"
Maisie laughed.

Daisy slowly peeped over the top of her book:
"It's all about bees.
Did you know that there are lots
of bees that live alone,
and they are called solitary bees."

Daisy explained happily,
"We helped Bombus the
bee by growing flowers
and built a pond for
Puddock the frog, so,
I thought I would learn
more. Look!" She turned
the book towards her
friends and showed
them a picture of a
red mason bee.

Red
Mason
Bee

Maisie looked confused, "It is called a red mason bee and yet it is not red, isn't that odd? Its furry bottom looks more ginger to me."

"It also looks quite different from Bombus, doesn't it? Mo observed, It has no yellow stripes and is smaller."

Buzz busy build

Buzz busy build

Buzz busy build

Maisie, Daisy, and Mo
suddenly stopped talking and looked at each other

What on earth was that noise?

Red
Mason
Bee

"It is a bee like the
red mason bee in the book,"
Daisy pointed to a page in her book.

The mason bee buzzed and hurried,
looking flustered and worried.

Maisie knelt next to the bee:
"Are you all right, little bee?
Would you like some help?"

"I'm Moira the red mason bee, and it's nice to meet you,
I do need some help. That is certainly true.
I can't find holes in those stems or that dead tree.
Can you find anything that would be useful for me?"

"We are Maisie, Daisy and Mo, and we would love to help you," smiled Maisie.

Thank you x

"Thank you, my friends. I shall buzz back later."
and off Moira flew.
Buzz, busy, build. Buzz, busy, build. Buzz, busy, build.

Maisie, Daisy and Mo looked confused.
"Moira told us she couldn't find any holes in plant stems
or dead tree wood. Let's find out what she uses them
for," suggested Daisy. She opened her book and they all
listened. "Mason bees use the holes to lay their eggs.
The good news is that if we can provide the right tubes,
the bees might be able to use them instead."
"But where will we find the right kind of tubes?" Mo asked.

"Let's go on a treasure hunt and bring back anything tube-shaped," suggested Maisie. Maisie, Daisy and Mo scattered in all directions. They searched in kitchen drawers, the garden shed, the storage cupboard, and their craft boxes.

Soon they returned with handfuls
of useful looking objects.

Mo picked up a straw, lifting it to his eye like a telescope. "This straw is nice and smooth, what do you think Daisy?"

Daisy inspected the straw, "I think it is too narrow for Moira to crawl inside although it might be good for other smaller bees."

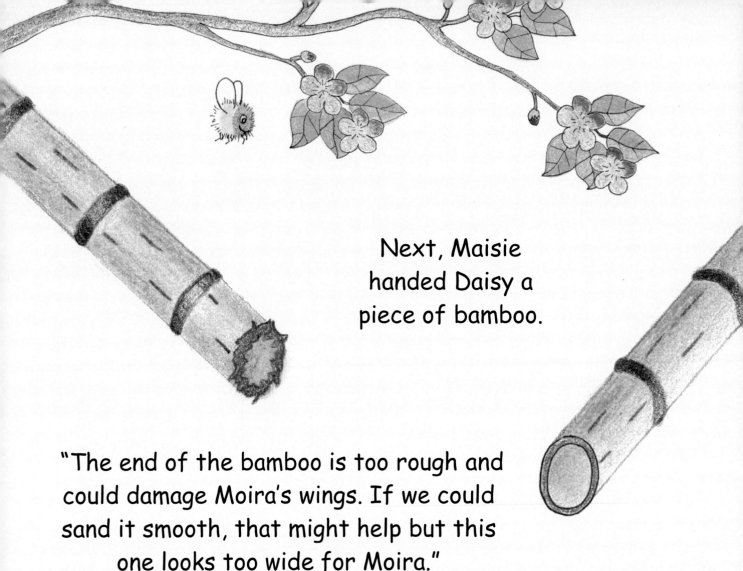

Next, Maisie
handed Daisy a
piece of bamboo.

"The end of the bamboo is too rough and
could damage Moira's wings. If we could
sand it smooth, that might help but this
one looks too wide for Moira."

Maisie looked disappointed, "This is difficult."

Maisie picked up a log,
"What about this,
it is like a very large tube shape?"

Daisy thought hard, "We could ask an adult to drill
holes in it and that might work, but it would be good
to have something we could show Moira today.
What else do we have?"

The last item in the pile
was a cardboard tube, like
a paper straw but slightly
shorter and a little wider.

Daisy looked at the tube from all sides and smiled.
"This cardboard tube is just right,
and I think it would be great for Moira."

Daisy picked up the book and read,
"The bee seals the end of the tube with mud,
lays her egg and puts in some pollen cake to
feed the larvae. That bed gets sealed with more mud
and the bee continues the process until the tube is full."

The female
mason bee
lays a single
egg in
each bed

Mo held up a bright blue box,
"This might be useful to hold the tubes and
they can be pushed snugly to the back of the box."
Maisie jumped up, overjoyed, "Let's call Moira."

Buzz busy build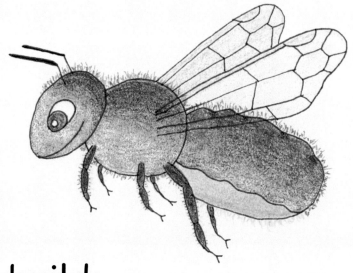

Buzz busy build

Buzz busy build

and Moira arrived.

"These are super smooth
tubes and just the right size,
And the box is just perfect.
You are all very wise.

Please place my box
with your flowers nearby,
As nectar and pollen
are a great food supply."

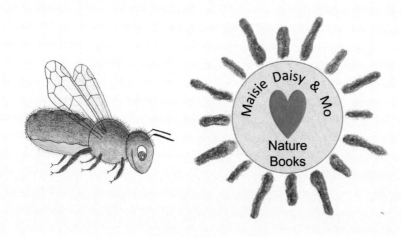

Moira buzzed, "My eggs
become larva, then pupa to bee.

This happens over winter,
so next spring, you will see

Lots of new
mason bees buzzing happily.
What a marvel of nature!
I hope you agree.

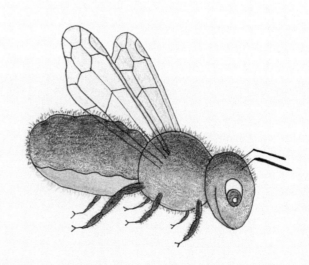

I must now fly, but thank you, my friends.

You have helped me so much.

I'll love you to the end."

Buzz busy build

Buzz busy build

Buzz busy build

and off Moira flew.

Next spring arrived,
and Maisie, Daisy and Mo were there.

Watching lots of new
bees fly around in the air.

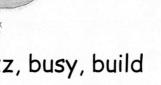

Buzz, busy, build. Buzz, busy, build. Buzz, busy, build
The baby bees buzzed, and everyone was thrilled.

Maisie, Daisy and Mo work best as a team,
Helping all wildlife and fulfilling their dream.
Let's all make a better world by hearing nature's call.
There's only one planet, and it's shared by us all.

Maisie, Daisy and Mo Extras

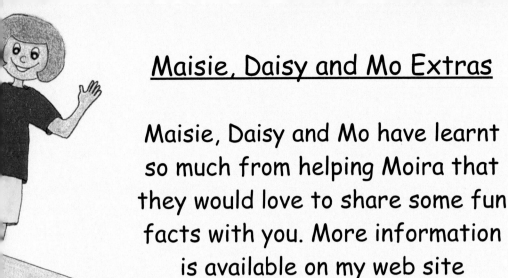

Maisie, Daisy and Mo have learnt so much from helping Moira that they would love to share some fun facts with you. More information is available on my web site www.bombusthebee.com

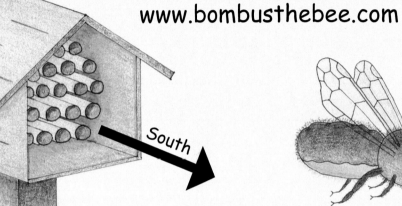

South

Mason bees break out of their cocoons in Spring when temperatures stay around 13°C, then it is 'Buzz, Busy, Build' time for mason bees like Moira.

The male bees appear from their cocoons first and are followed a week or two later by the females. It is so clever that the red mason bees lay the female eggs at the back of the tube and the males at the front.

Mason bees are described as cavity nesting bees which means they make their bee beds in hollows that they find in the wild. These can be in plant stems, holes in dead wood or crumbling mortar in old walls. Sometimes they have difficulty finding these and then we can help, like Maisie, Daisy and Mo have in the story.

Mason bees prefer a tube length of at least 15cm with an internal diameter of about 8 mm. The tube shown on this page is roughly the correct size.

The back end of the tubes is best blocked off and, in this story, Maisie, Daisy and Mo suggest pushing the tubes snuggly to the back of a box. The box should be positioned in a warm spot facing roughly south, like the picture above. The box should be over 1 metre above ground level. Ensure the front of the box has an overhang to keep the tubes dry. Ideally the box can be opened for thorough cleaning at the end of the season, once all the tubes are removed.

The female bees use clay rich mud to build their bee beds.

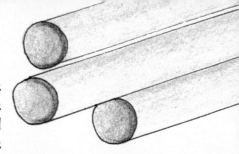

The mason bee starts by blocking the far end of the tube with the clay mud and once this is done the bee collects nectar and pollen. The bee enters the tube head first and regurgitates the nectar on to the clay. The bee leaves the tube and then enters backwards and scrapes off the pollen which was collected on its hairs. The pollen and nectar get mixed together and makes a pollen cake.

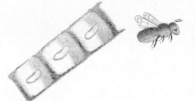

The egg is then laid on the pollen cake and the bed sealed with more mud and this process is repeated until the tube is full. The final mud cap is extra thick to protect the precious eggs behind.

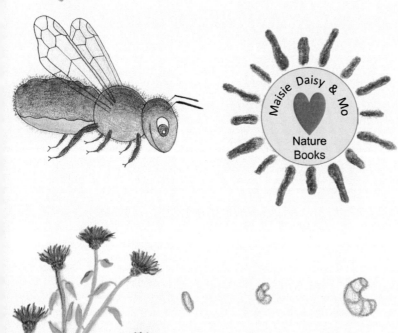

The egg is about the size of a grain of rice. The eggs hatch into larvae and feed on the pollen cake and once it has all been eaten, they spin a cocoon. The pupa develops inside the cocoon and slowly becomes a bee. Throughout the winter the bees are dormant (asleep) within their cocoons. Then in spring it all begins again.

 It can take over 250 visits to build up enough food for a tube of bee beds, a lot of work for our busy bee.

Buzz
Busy
Build

There are around 250 different types of solitary bees in the UK and over 20,000 worldwide. Most solitary bees are ground-nesting and burrow into the ground to make their nests. But some species are cavity-nesters.

In addition to red mason bees, you are likely to get leafcutter bees visiting your bee hotel and if you are lucky, you may see it carrying a leaf. You may also see orange-vented mason bees and blue mason bees that plug their nest with pieces of chewed up leaves, as well as smaller yellow-face bees.

 Bees are very important pollinators because the pollen that is trapped on the hairs on their body and then falls off on each flower as they fly between them.

 Bees collect lots of pollen and nectar from flowers, which is why we need to provide lots of pollinator friendly flowers in our gardens. Please see my other book Bombus and the Beeline.

As a rough guide the more open the flower bloom is, then the more accessible the pollen and nectar are for the bees.

My favourite, tried and tested plant is cat mint (not cat nip) and there are lots more plants that I have tried at www.bombusthebee.com